RED ALERT

BOOKS IN THE PUPPY PATROL SERIES ™

COMING SOON

PUPPY PATROL ™

RED ALERT

JENNY DALE

Illustrations by Mick Reid
Cover illustration by Michael Rowe

AN
APPLE
PAPERBACK

SCHOLASTIC INC.
New York Toronto London Auckland Sydney
Mexico City New Delhi Hong Kong

ISBN 0-439-21810-1

24 23 22 21 20 19 18 17 16 15 14 13   4 5 6/0

Printed in the U.S.A.   40
First Scholastic printing, January 2001

SPECIAL THANKS TO CHERITH BALDRY

CHAPTER ONE

"**H**as anyone seen Dad?" asked Neil Parker as he breezed into the kitchen of his home at King Street Kennels and dropped his backpack on the floor. "One of the kids at school was asking about bringing her dog to the next obedience class."

Neil's nine-year-old sister, Emily, was sitting at the big wooden table in the center of the room, chewing the end of a pencil. Spread out in front of her was a mountain of math homework. Her mother was helping her. Before answering Neil's question, Mrs. Parker tapped Emily's book and remarked, "When I was at school, seven sevens didn't make fifty-nine."

"Oops," said Emily, erasing her mistake.

Carole Parker looked up. "That shouldn't be a

problem, Neil. Your father's outside in the kennel somewhere."

"He's settling in the new dogs," Emily added.

"New dogs?" Neil grinned. He loved life at the kennel and the thought of new dogs for him to get to know put everything else out of his mind.

Without looking up, Emily said, "He was in the rescue center fifteen minutes ago. But you could try the barn — I think he wanted to straighten up after last night's class." Then she returned to the complexities of her homework.

Neil lived on the outskirts of the small country town of Compton. His mother and father ran a boarding kennel and a rescue center for stray dogs. Everybody in Compton knew about King Street Kennels — or the "Puppy Patrol," as Neil's friends called the Parkers.

Neil stepped outside onto the garden path leading toward the kennels and looked around. Straight ahead, across the courtyard between the two kennel blocks, there was no sign of his father. He looked over at the barn on his left, and beyond that toward the rescue center, but there was no sign of life.

Neil whistled and Sam, his black-and-white Border collie, came racing up from his favorite place under the hedge in the garden.

"Hi there, Sam," Neil said, ruffling the collie's ears. "Have you seen Dad?"

Sam panted happily and his tail wagged with excitement. He followed Neil over to the converted barn where Bob Parker gave his twice-weekly obedience classes. Neil pushed one of the tall wooden doors open and called out, "Dad! Are you in here?"

His voice echoed among the wooden beams high in the roof, but there was no reply. Neil peered through the gloom inside and saw nothing except the heaped bales of straw they used for the dogs' bedding at the far end.

He pulled the door shut behind him and walked across the grass between the barn and the rescue center. A small block of ten pens standing on the far

side of the barn, the rescue center offered its temporary guests as much comfort as the pens in the kennel blocks. Every dog had a comfortable basket, some doggie toys, and the use of an outside run for exercise.

Kate McGuire, the Parkers' kennel assistant, was preparing one of the pens for a new arrival. She was a tall, thin girl with blond hair in a ponytail. She loved her job and was a natural with dogs.

"Hi, Kate," said Neil, greeting her with a smile. "Have you seen my dad around? And who's the pen for?"

Kate straightened up and wiped her hands on the front of her yellow sweatshirt. "Your father's in the exercise field," she replied, then gave Neil a mischievous grin. "But as to who our new visitor is, you'll have to wait and see. It's a surprise!"

Neil frowned but he knew Kate too well to try to get an answer out of her. As he puzzled over who the visitor might be, he peered into the pen nearest the door. In it was a mutt puppy the Parkers had named Blackie. She came bouncing up to the mesh screen as Neil approached her.

"Blackie! Hasn't Kate been paying you enough attention?" Neil laughed and fished in his pocket for one of the dog treats he always carried. Blackie gulped it down and looked at him for more. Neil rubbed her nose through the mesh. "Not just now," he said, smiling.

In another pen was a springer spaniel, asleep in her basket. Next to her was a German shepherd who Bob said had an unpredictable temper. Neil wondered if it was because the dog was unhappy in these strange surroundings. Nevertheless, Neil had to be careful near him, so he quickly slipped a dog treat through the mesh of the dog's pen and stood back.

"Any sign of this one's owner, Kate?"

Kate joined him and shook her head. "Not yet. But your dad has given the police a description of the dog." She moved along to another pen and peered in. "Come take a look, Neil. This is the little fella I'm really worried about."

Huddled in one corner of the pen was a dog Neil had not seen before — a small brown mutt with a smooth coat. Neil squatted down. "Hello, boy," he said. "What's your name? Here." He held out a treat, but the dog didn't come any closer to take it. Instead the animal whimpered softly and looked up at Neil with liquid, miserable eyes.

"Hey," said Neil quietly, "there's nothing to be scared of. No one's going to hurt you."

Sam nosed at Neil's hand, demanding a treat of his own. Neil grinned at him and gave in but his attention stayed on the mutt in the pen. The dog didn't look as if it had been abused, but something had happened to make him very nervous.

"I can't remember when I last saw a dog as jumpy as that," Kate said.

"Don't worry, boy." Neil dropped the treat through the wire. "We'll take care of you," he promised.

He said good-bye to the mutt and followed Kate out of the rescue center, closing the door behind him.

"I'm finished for the day," said Kate.

"Date tonight?" Neil asked, grinning.

Kate laughed. "Ha! No chance! I'm going to put my feet up with a good book, actually!"

Neil smiled and waved good-bye to her as she rode off on her bike. Ambling over to the gate of the exercise field that bordered the kennels, he wondered who the new rescue center dog was.

Bob Parker was in the field and had just thrown a stick for the dog with him. The dog streaked off in pursuit of the stick. Neil recognized the animal as an Irish setter. It ran with a beautiful, flowing movement and as the rays of the setting sun caught the dog's coat it made the silky hair look as if it were on fire. Neil gave a soft whistle of admiration as the setter retrieved the stick and bounded up to Bob, its tail waving in the breeze. Bob took the stick, patted the setter's back, and slipped it a dog treat, before getting ready to throw the stick again.

"Dad!" Neil called. "Over here!"

His father turned and saw him, then walked over to the gate, the Irish setter trotting obediently at his heel.

Bob Parker was a big man, broad shouldered, with a thatch of brown hair. Dogs were his life, too, but al-

though Neil knew how much he cared about them, he had not often seen his father looking at a dog with the interest and pride he was showing toward the setter.

"He's beautiful!" Neil exclaimed as Bob brought the setter into the garden and closed the gate behind them. "Where did you get him?" He squatted down and held out a hand for the Irish setter to sniff. Looking at the dog more closely, Neil realized that he had seen him before. "This is Red, isn't it? Is he boarding with us again?"

At first, Bob Parker didn't answer Neil's question. He was too busy watching as Red and Sam looked each other over. Red had been Bob Parker's very first boarder, when he and Carole had set up King Street Kennels over ten years ago. Red had boarded with them several times since then, and Neil had gotten to know the handsome dog. Over the years, Bob had become friendly with his owner, Jim Birchall. As Red nudged and nuzzled the Border collie, Neil could tell that he was obviously a happy, friendly creature with no problem at all being with other dogs.

Together Neil and his father walked back toward the kennel blocks, the two dogs side by side behind them.

"Kate's prepared a pen in the rescue center, Dad. Who's that for, then? Red isn't a rescue dog."

"He is now, Neil," Bob said, his expression becoming more serious. "I'm afraid Jim Birchall died on Tuesday. He had a heart attack. It was completely unexpected."

"Oh." Neil felt shocked and didn't really know what to say. Jim Birchall had never seemed that old to him. He was always so full of life and he used to walk Red for miles every day.

"Jim's sister knew that Red and I had always gotten along well," Bob continued, "so she called me at lunchtime and asked if I would take him."

"What? She didn't want to keep him?" Neil asked in disbelief.

"She can't stand dogs, I'm afraid," Bob said.

"Nasty, dirty animals according to her." He grinned briefly. "I thought she would disinfect me before she let me set foot in the house. So it looks like we'll have to find another home for Red."

"A really good one," Neil said.

"The best."

In the rescue center, Bob led Red into the pen next to the small brown mutt. Red nosed around interestedly.

"We should be OK with Red, Neil. He's very friendly and wouldn't have much trouble settling in somewhere new," said Bob. "But this little guy's another story." He stuck his hands into the pockets of his shabby corduroy pants and looked down at the mutt. The dog was still crouched in the far corner of his pen, and the treat that Neil had left earlier was still lying untouched.

"A couple brought him in this morning," Bob explained. "They found him sniffing around their garden. They live miles from anywhere so it looks as if he might have been abandoned deliberately." His voice grew angry. Nothing much bothered Neil's father except for a dog being ill-treated. "I don't know what they've done to him, but he's incredibly nervous. He won't come to me, he won't eat, and he doesn't want to play. He just sits and shivers."

As Neil and Bob watched, Red finished investigating his own pen. He trotted over to the mesh that separated his pen from that of the mutt and gave a soft, inviting whine. The mutt lifted his head but didn't move out of the corner.

"We'll leave them to get to know each other," Bob said, leading the way out of the rescue center. "By the way, Neil, do you want to give the mutt a name?"

Neil thought about it for a moment. "Why not call him Brownie?" he suggested. "He's just the right color."

"Red's settling in well," Bob said as he sank into his favorite chair in the Parkers' living room with the *Compton News* in his hand. He paused before opening it and said, "You know, I've been thinking . . ."

"What about?" Carole asked.

"About Red. What would you think, all of you, if we gave him a new home here?"

Emily looked up from her animal magazine, bright-eyed.

Sarah, Neil's youngest sister, who was playing with Sam on the fireplace rug, squealed, "Oh, yes, he's so great!"

Neil said nothing, but he felt a smile beginning to form on his lips.

"Are you sure, Bob?" asked Carole. "We always said we wouldn't take any dogs from the rescue center."

"We took Sam," Neil said.

The Parkers had found Sam abandoned as a puppy when Neil was seven. He had become Neil's dog — and his special friend. No other dog could ever take Sam's place for Neil, but he liked Red's confident, outgoing nature, and he knew that his father was very close to the Irish setter.

"Sam is one dog, Neil," Carole said. "If we're not careful, we could be knee-deep in them. I know what you're all like."

Sarah gave a wide smile. "Oh, yes!" she sighed happily. "Lots and lots of dogs!"

Carole shuddered and covered her eyes with one hand. "Lots of dogs? It's hard enough having three children! Don't even think about it!"

"But Red's not just any dog," said Bob. "We know him well, he was our first-ever guest — so he's special. Besides . . ." He paused again.

"What is it, Dad?" Emily asked anxiously.

"Red's active, but he's not a young dog. He won't live for more than a couple of years — three at most. I'd like to think that I'd looked after him when he needed me."

Carole scanned the faces around the room.

"We'll all help," said Neil. "I can walk him when I walk Sam. They've already been making friends with each other. You'll enjoy having somebody to play with, won't you, Sam?"

Sam gave a bark of approval and thumped his tail on the floor.

"I can groom him," Emily added. "I'm learning how."

Carole started to laugh. "You're all against me, I can see!" she said. "Well, OK. After all, what are rules for if not to be broken every now and then?"

Sarah and Emily both started clapping. Neil couldn't help jumping up, punching the air, and shouting, "Yes!" Then an idea came to him. "Mom," he said, grinning, "will you come into school and say that bit about breaking rules to my teacher, Mr. Hamley?"

Before Neil went to sleep he thought about having another dog in the family. Red was beautiful, lively, and intelligent. He couldn't think of a better addition to the Parker home. Neil rolled his blanket around him like a cocoon and switched off the bedside light.

Neil went to sleep and dreamed of dogs — big dogs, small dogs, red dogs, black-and-white dogs, and even bright green dogs with yellow spots. They were all racing around him; he was knee-deep in dogs, just as his mother had said. And they were all barking. Neil didn't know whether to push them off or hug them. He wondered what would happen if a million dogs sat on you all at once.

He jerked awake to find that the barking was real. Every dog in the kennel seemed to be joining in. Instead of morning, an uncertain red light was flickering in through his window.

Neil groped his way to the window and pulled back the curtains. His room overlooked the courtyard, where everything was dark. The red light was coming from his left, and when Neil opened his window and leaned out, he could see flames leaping up from the roof of the barn.

Neil stared. For a few seconds he was frozen with shock. Then he dashed across his room, picked up his jeans, and flung the door open.

"Mom! Dad!" he yelled out. "Wake up! Quick, the barn's on fire!"

CHAPTER TWO

"**N**eil? What's the matter?" Carole Parker's voice was fuzzy with sleep as she emerged from her bedroom.

"The barn's on fire!" Neil cried urgently as he stumbled downstairs to the telephone while pulling a sweater over his head. As he dialed 911, lights went on all over the house as his parents sprang into action.

"Emergency. Which service, please?"

The calm voice of the operator steadied Neil as he stood in the hallway taking deep breaths. "Fire!" he gasped. As Neil answered the vital questions, Bob and Carole Parker swept past him and into the kitchen. He heard the back door slam as somebody ran outside.

Neil hung up the phone and ran to the kitchen. Through the window blinds he could see a shimmering red-and-yellow glow.

"Well done, Neil," said Carole as she hurriedly tied her shoelaces.

Neil moved toward the kitchen door but Carole reached out and held him back. "No," she said. "You stay here."

"But, Mom . . ."

Bob reappeared, bringing the smell of smoke with him, and interrupted Neil. He spoke rapidly but calmly. "The wind's blowing away from the house. I think the kennel blocks are safe, but the flames could reach the rescue center. We need to get the dogs out. Fast!"

"Mom?" Emily's voice drifted down to them from the top of the stairs. "Mom, what's happening?"

"Stay inside, Emily. Make sure Sarah doesn't come downstairs," Carole said. "We have to move some of the dogs."

Neil suddenly felt his father's firm hand on his arm. "Come with me, Neil. But be careful. Stay away from the flames."

"OK. I . . . I will." Neil pushed his feet into his sneakers, leaving the laces dangling, grabbed his jacket, and followed his father into the peculiar warmth outside.

"Make sure that Sam stays indoors, too," shouted Carole Parker as she went to close the door behind her. Then she paused and added, "And Emily, call Mike Turner. We might be needing a vet."

Neil plunged out into the whirling ash and scraps of charred debris that filled the air. The smell of smoke assaulted his nostrils and he could hear the crackle of the fire and feel waves of heat on his face.

Flames from the roof of the barn licked at the dark sky, sending up billows of smoke flecked with sparks. It looked like the biggest bonfire Neil had ever seen. The far end of the barn was covered with flames and the yellow tongues of fire were being carried away from the house toward the rescue center by the strong night wind.

He raced past the barn and into the rescue center. The air was hazy with smoke, driving the dogs into a panic and causing them to bark frantically. Bob had the German shepherd out of his pen and on a leash.

". . . dangerous if he's loose," he was saying, almost shouting to make himself heard over the terrified animals. "I'll put him in the spare pen in Block One." He led the dog out; it snarled and pulled against its leash.

Carole rushed past and opened Blackie's pen. She grabbed the squirming puppy and thrust her into Neil's hands. "Put her in the house," she said urgently. "Emily can watch her."

Neil shoved the little dog inside his jacket and sprinted back to the kitchen. Sarah was sitting on the floor with one arm around her teddy bear and the other around Sam. The dog sprang to its feet as soon as Neil came over. In the passageway he could hear Emily talking on the phone.

"No, Sam," Neil commanded. "Sit. Stay."

Sam sat obediently, but he looked disappointed. Neil extracted the wriggling Blackie from his jacket and put her on the floor beside Sarah. "Here, Squirt, have a puppy."

Sarah beamed with delight and let Blackie climb into her lap. Neil rushed out again, batting at the sparks that swirled into his face. The smoke was thickening and beginning to sting his eyes.

In the rescue center, there was no sign of Bob or Carole. The spaniel's pen was empty; Neil guessed that his mother had already taken her to the kennel. Neil took down the leash that hung outside Red's pen, opened the door, and went to get the setter. Red

was on his feet, barking furiously, but he grew quiet as soon as Neil touched him and clipped on the leash. "Good boy," Neil said soothingly. "Good boy, Red."

He led the Irish setter out and opened Brownie's pen. The little mutt was huddled in the far corner, whimpering pitifully. "It's OK, boy," Neil said reassuringly. "I've come to get you out."

As he struggled to hold Red and pick up the frightened mutt, Emily arrived, panting and coughing in the smoke-filled air.

"Give Red to me, Neil. Mike's on his way," she said before he had a chance to argue.

Neil gratefully thrust the leash into Emily's outstretched hands and went over to Brownie. As he bent down, the dog bared his teeth viciously. The mutt growled, pricked up his ears, and as Neil drew back, startled, Brownie slipped past him and dashed out of the pen.

"Brownie!" Neil shouted. "Come here!"

It was no use. Barking frantically, Brownie disappeared through the outer door. Neil started to chase the dog and Emily rushed out after them, clutching Red's leash firmly in her hands.

Outside, in the red light of the flames, Neil saw Brownie racing toward the house. Neil bolted after him. Then his mother appeared, her tall figure glowing orange from the light of the flames, running toward the barn with a fire extinguisher in her hands.

"Catch Brownie!" Neil yelled out to her.

Carole put the fire extinguisher down and went after the mutt as he came toward her, but Brownie was too fast for her. He dodged her grasping hands and changed direction. The little dog streaked past the barn into the darker shadows near the house and almost tripped Neil's dad as he came around the corner from the kennel blocks. Still barking in a frenzy, Brownie doubled back toward the barn. Neil sprinted and caught up with him but the dog veered away.

"Head him off!" Neil yelled to Emily, waving his arms.

Emily flung herself at Brownie. Her feet caught in Red's leash, and the setter jerked it out of her grip. For a second, Neil thought Emily was going to catch him, but the terrified dog slipped through her hands. Emily stumbled to the floor and Brownie, desperate to escape, vanished through the doorway of the blazing barn.

"Brownie!" The barking of the dogs and crackle of the flames bombarded Neil's ears. Without thinking, he followed Brownie into the barn.

Thick smoke was heavy in the air and Neil could barely see. A dull red glow came from the far end.

The roar of the fire was deafening in his ears and he could neither see Brownie nor hear him.

"Brownie! Brownie!" he called. He wished he knew the dog's real name. He might come for that. "Here, boy! Here, boy!"

There was no response.

Neil moved forward tentatively, trying to see through the billowing smoke. His eyes were streaming and he coughed as the smoke tortured his throat. The heat was growing more intense as the fire crept toward him down the length of the barn.

Then, above the crackling of the fire, he heard Brownie's frightened whimpering, somewhere over to his right. Bending over, sweeping his hands back and forth at floor level, Neil moved toward the sound. He tried calling to the dog again but his words were lost in a fit of coughing.

The whimpering stopped and Neil started to wonder if he would ever find Brownie. But just then, one of his groping hands touched a smooth, healthy coat. He heard Brownie's claws scrabble on the floor, but before the dog could escape him again, Neil gripped his collar. "Crazy mutt," he said, choking.

Neil was shaking, yet relieved. Tucking Brownie under his arm, he got to his feet and turned toward the door. Then he stopped. All around him was smoke and the lurid glow of the flames. He could not tell which way the door was.

Fear hit Neil for the first time. He had been worried about Brownie, but not about his own safety. Now he turned his head left and right, trying to force his stinging eyes to peer through the smoke and find the way out.

The fire had spread rapidly in the hurried seconds he had been looking for Brownie. Flames seemed to be reaching at him from all directions. Neil thought of his mother with the fire extinguisher and knew that it wouldn't be any use against this.

He turned in what he thought might be the right direction and took a few steps, but the heat drove him back. He used his free arm to shield his eyes and tried to shout, to tell his mom and dad where he was, but all he could manage was to cough violently. He picked up a muffled sound but could not tell what direction it came from.

Then he heard a dog barking close by. Not Brownie, who was shivering under his arm, but a loud, commanding bark from somewhere else. He heard it again, closer still, and Neil saw Red appear through the swirling smoke, his healthy coat glinting in the light of the flames.

"Red!"

The setter swiped a warm, rough tongue over Neil's hand, and Neil, blinking away the smoke, tried to pat him. "Have you come to save me?"

Red fastened his teeth in the bottom of Neil's jacket and began tugging him gently.

Neil let Red pull him, and he stumbled forward to what he hoped would be safety. The smoke began to clear and the large, dark shape of a familiar figure loomed up at him, a handkerchief tied over its nose and mouth. Bob Parker grabbed his son and shouted, "I've got him!"

Seconds later, Neil was stumbling out of the barn and into the courtyard beyond. He doubled over, coughed, and took in huge lungfuls of the crisp, fresh air.

"Neil, are you all right?" Emily asked anxiously.

"Don't you ever do anything so unsafe again, Neil!" shouted his mother. Then her arms were around him and she was hugging him.

Suddenly there was a loud roar and a surge of flames as part of the barn's roof collapsed in on itself.

The gust of smoke and heat sent the group of figures running farther away from the flames toward the house.

For once, Neil was happy just to be hugged, but after a few seconds he realized that Brownie was wriggling frantically. He pulled back and turned to Bob. His father had used a rope as a lifeline so that he and Neil could find their way out of the smoke-filled barn. He was now coiling up the blackened rope.

"Look, Dad, I have Brownie!"

"I know, Neil," Bob said tensely, "but it was still a crazy thing to do. Not even a dog is worth your life."

"I know that and if Red hadn't —" Neil stopped talking when he heard the wail of a siren approaching up the road from Compton. It grew louder with every passing second, and a moment later, a fire engine swept into the driveway, its siren still blaring and lights flashing. Several firefighters poured from it and erupted into purposeful action.

The Parkers stepped back to give them space to work. There was no need to say anything, but they had to keep watching. Bob wiped his face with his handkerchief. As well as being covered with smudges of black ash, his forehead was cut and a tiny stream of blood trickled from it. The palms of Emily's hands were grazed where she had fallen while trying to catch Brownie, and Neil could feel his cheeks and arms tingling with the fiery sensation of having been so close to the flames. Neil gradually realized the danger he had been in.

Standing in the silence watching the firefighters work, the tight knot of fear Neil had felt began to relax, and he sensed a surge of relief that all the dogs had been successfully rescued. Now that the emergency services were on hand, the fire would not spread any farther. The jets of water dulled the rampant flames; already their yellow glow was beginning to fade.

But suddenly Neil knew there was something wrong. A dog was missing.

"Dad," he said, urgently turning and gripping his father's arm. "Have you seen Red? Did you see where he went?"

Bob Parker shook his head and quickly glanced around. Carole and Emily began peering in all directions, too.

"He came after me and saved my life. If it hadn't been for him . . ."

Neil scanned the area around the fire engine but there was no sign of Red. Slowly, and not wanting to bring himself to face the thought that had now crept into his mind, Neil looked toward the burning barn.

"Red?"

CHAPTER THREE

Neil saw the silhouettes of the firefighters against the fading red glow of the smoldering barn. The wreckage was crackling and sizzling as they directed their strong jets of water onto the barn. Neil looked around frantically but there was no sign of Red.

Bob whistled and called out, "Red! Red!"

"We've got to find him!" Neil said.

"I'll go," said Bob. He ran off in the direction of the fire. Neil could hear him shouting the dog's name as he went.

Neil realized that he was still clutching Brownie. The timid dog was calm, except for a faint trembling, and was breathing as if he was exhausted. Neil shifted to try to make the little dog more comfortable in his arms and stroked his sleek head.

"Cheer up, boy," he said. "It's not your fault, is it?"

"Give him to me," Carole said. "I have to go in and check on Sarah. The two of you stay with your father. Watch yourselves — the barn is still dangerous."

The fire was almost out. The clamor of barking from the kennel blocks was beginning to die down but wisps of smoke still lingered in the air, and the smell of burned, wet wood clung to Neil's and Emily's clothes as they walked toward the wreckage. Dark heaps of charred wood and jagged stumps were all that remained of the King Street Kennels barn.

Neil suddenly realized how tired he felt. His whole body ached and his throat was still sore from the effects of breathing in smoke. He forced himself into action, stumbling toward the scattered wreckage but staying clear of the crumpled barn structure, dodging the fire hoses that snaked across the ground. Emily walked alongside him and together they splashed through the pools of water and mashed half-burned straw and wads of soggy, blackened newspaper into the soft earth.

After drenching the last remnants of the blaze, the firefighters were beginning to clear out their equipment.

"Don't touch anything," one of them said to Neil and Emily as they went past.

Neil could see his father poking around in some wreckage a couple of yards away from the far end of the barn where the blaze had been strongest. Clearly he hadn't found Red yet. Neil felt that something was very wrong. If nothing was the matter with Red, he would be here. Either he had run off, or he was lying injured somewhere, or dead. Neil didn't want to think the worst.

He and Emily spread out to search the ground nearby, in between the barn and the rescue center. It would be a while before anyone could dig around in the ruins themselves to see if Red was buried there. Neil looked for a glimpse of Red's bright chestnut coat.

He had only been looking for a few minutes when he heard a car approaching. He hoped it was Mike Turner, but when he looked toward the driveway by the side of the house he saw the flashing blue light of a police car.

He saw his father making his way toward the gate. Maybe it was too much to hope that Mike Turner would come so soon. The vet had his office in Compton, but he lived in the nearby town of Padsham, so it would take him a while to drive the several miles from his home.

Neil went on searching the blackened grass around the remains of the barn.

Then Neil heard Emily gasp. She was looking at a small, dark heap on the ground. At first he thought it was one more piece of debris but he trudged over to where she was standing and bent down. It was Red.

Neil could hardly believe the change. The setter lay still on the wet ground. His coat was soaked through and caked into spikes from ash and debris. Instead of chestnut, the color of his fur was almost black. A heavy piece of wood had fallen away from the disintegrating barn wall and across his hindquarters, pinning him to the ground.

Emily shouted out for help and Bob soon came running over to the same spot. Bob quickly heaved the timber away and knelt in the mud beside Red. As he reached out to touch the setter's muzzle, the dog stirred, whimpered, and tried to lift his head. Neil felt a weak smile spreading across his face.

"He's alive!"

"But hurt," Bob said gravely.

Red was trying to pull himself to his feet. He raised himself on his forelegs but his hindquarters were scrabbling uselessly. After a short struggle he flopped back into the mud.

Bob laid a hand gently on the dog's flank. Red was panting and obviously in great pain after his efforts to move. The dog's coat around his stomach area was bloody.

"Steady, boy," said Bob. "Lie still. Neil, go and get —"

The sound of another car driving up beside the house caught their attention.

"That could be Mike!" Emily said. "I'll go and check."

She ran off toward the gate, and came back a moment later with the vet striding behind her with his emergency first-aid kit. Mike Turner's usually cheerful face showed shock.

"I got here as quickly as I could," he said as he approached. He squatted down beside Red and quickly felt along the dog's limbs and body with his expert hands. Red remained still, whimpering occasionally, while Neil and the others waited tensely for Mike's verdict.

"Not good," Mike said at last. The vet stood up and rubbed his sleepy eyes. "His back leg's broken but I'm afraid that might be the least of his worries. He's suffered an injury to the area near his stomach. There could be internal injuries and possibly some damage to his spine."

"You mean it's broken?" Neil whispered.

"I can't say. I'll have to do a thorough examination at the hospital before I can be sure. But there's the cold as well and the massive shock to his system, the smoke . . ."

"Will he live?" asked Emily.

Mike paused. "Well, I hate to say this . . . but the kindest thing might be to put him to sleep. Bob?"

"No!" Bob protested firmly. "We've got to try . . ."

Neil couldn't remember ever seeing his father looking so upset. He cared for all dogs but this was just more proof that Red meant something special to him. His throat still dry, Neil rasped, "He saved my life. In the barn."

Mike looked at him, not understanding, but not questioning him, either. "OK," he said matter-of-factly. "We fight." He rested a hand on the setter's head. "Are you a fighter, boy?"

Two police officers shone powerful flashlights over the smoldering remains of the barn as they asked Bob about what had happened. Mike Turner splintered Red's injured leg and wrapped him warmly in blankets. Neil helped carry the setter to the vet's car. As they were making Red comfortable, Carole came out of the house.

"I'll put him in the intensive care unit, Carole," Mike said. "I'll do everything I can. But he's in bad shape. Please don't expect too much."

"Of course, Mike, thank you. But there's another dog I want you to look at. He's in the kitchen. Can you spare a couple of minutes?"

Neil and Emily followed their mother and Mike inside. Brownie was lying in the old basket chair by the kitchen window, panting miserably.

"He's probably inhaled too much smoke," said Mike after a quick examination. "I'll take him with me, too. I don't think it's anything serious, but I'll keep him under observation for twenty-four hours to be sure."

Neil coughed as he heard the good news. It would have been terrible if another dog had suffered because of the fire.

Carole looked at him, a concerned expression on her face. "I'd better get you taken care of, too, Neil. You don't sound very healthy, either."

When Mike had gone, the Parkers tried to relax after their exhausting ordeal. The firefighters had left, the police had marked off the area of the burnt barn for further examination in the morning, and all the dogs in the rescue center were accounted for. Both the spaniel and the bad-tempered German shepherd were temporarily housed in spare pens in the kennel blocks but there was no more space for Blackie, so she stayed indoors as an emergency house pet. Bob said he would move them all back later in the day, after he had checked the rescue center for possible damage, when it was light out.

Carole promised Neil that she would get Dr. Harvey out the following morning to check out his cough. Neil protested that he was all right, but he knew that he would have to endure an examination eventually and grudgingly agreed.

Carole sent him and Emily to take showers before they went back to bed. As Neil put on his pajamas he could hear one or two of the dogs still howling outside. Memories of Red came flooding back to him. He thought about how the brave dog had dragged him from the burning barn and then how pathetic he had looked lying injured and bandaged in the back of Mike Turner's car. Neil thought he would be far too worried about Red to sleep at all but he crashed into unconsciousness as soon as he crawled into bed.

When Neil woke up, sunlight was streaming into his bedroom. He washed halfheartedly, dragged his clothes on, and, yawning, made his way to the kitchen. To his surprise, the room was empty except for Sam, lying on the floor while Blackie climbed enthusiastically all over him. Sam lifted his head and gave Neil a look, as if he wanted to say, "Don't tell anyone you saw me doing this."

Neil smiled and looked to see if anyone was around when Carole appeared from the direction of the office. "Any news about Red?" he asked immediately.

Carole shook her head.

Neil followed her back into the kitchen. "Where is everybody? And what's for breakfast?"

"You mean, what's for lunch," his mother said. "It's nearly twelve."

Neil stood with his mouth open. "But I'm late for school! Mr. Hamley will be furious."

Neil's teacher at Meadowbank School was a stickler for punctuality and was often called Smiler — because he didn't.

"Don't worry," Carole told him. "I called your school. The principal said you all should stay home today. He understands the situation here. I've arranged for the doctor to come by later this afternoon."

Neil shrugged. "Great," he said sarcastically. "At least that means we can help out around the kennels today."

"That should please Kate," Carole said, smiling. "She's already done wonders this morning, but she hasn't had time to walk all the dogs. When Emily gets up you could both give your dad a hand, too. He's been cleaning up the rescue center. I don't think he slept at all last night."

Neil poured himself a glass of milk and drank it quickly, then slapped together a peanut-butter-and-jelly sandwich to eat on the way out.

"Come on, boy," he said to Sam. "Time for a walk. You've done enough baby-sitting for now."

Neil crossed the courtyard with Sam at his heels, intending to go and look for Kate, but the first person he saw was his father, ushering a man toward the flattened site of the barn. The stranger was tall, thin, and gray-haired. He was wearing a conservative suit and carrying a briefcase. Neil was curious, changed direction, and followed them.

"I have no idea," Bob was saying as Neil came into earshot. "The barking woke up my son in the middle of the night and he got the rest of us up. The barn was in flames by then, unfortunately."

"That's right," Neil said loudly.

The strange man turned around and looked at him with a thin, disapproving face.

"Neil, this is Mr. Pye from the insurance company," Bob said. "He wants to confirm what happened last night."

Mr. Pye put down his briefcase, took out a clipboard, and made a note. "So you have no idea how the fire started? Hmmm . . ." He walked on toward the wreckage, picking his way carefully between the puddles in his polished shoes. Bob and Neil followed. Neil saw that his father was looking worried.

Mr. Pye stopped at the edge of the blackened shell of the barn, peered at it, and made more notes.

Neil stared at it, too. In the daylight, Neil could see the extent of the devastation more clearly. The barn had folded in on itself, and where the large building had once towered above his head, the highest point of the barn was now no higher than his waist.

"What was the building used for?" asked Mr. Pye, interrupting Neil's thoughts.

"Mostly for the obedience classes," Bob said. He explained how dog owners brought their dogs to the kennels for training twice a week. "And partly for storage," he finished.

"Storage of what?"

"Straw for the dogs' bedding," Bob replied. "And some old newspapers."

"All highly flammable, Mr. Parker," Mr. Pye said. "One spark and the whole thing would go up. As it did."

"I've been inspected for fire safety," Bob said.

"No doubt. No doubt. And where did the spark come from, hmm? What about these people who come for the classes? Could any of them have dropped a cigarette?"

"The last class was on Wednesday evening," Bob replied. "Over twenty-four hours before the fire started. Besides, smoking isn't allowed in the barn or anywhere else on these premises. I make that very clear to all our customers."

"I see." Mr. Pye suddenly turned to face Neil. "And what about you, young man? No quick cigarettes where your father wouldn't see you, eh?"

"No!" Neil felt himself flush red with indignation. "I don't smoke. And even if I did, I wouldn't be stupid enough to smoke on a pile of straw!"

Bob put a hand on Neil's shoulder. It said, *Keep calm,* as clearly as if he had spoken.

"Mr. Pye, I'm as puzzled as you are about the fire," said Bob.

"Hmm . . ." Mr. Pye transferred his inquisitive gaze back to Bob. "Business doing well, is it, Mr. Parker? No financial problems? Outstanding debts?"

Neil didn't understand the question, but he realized that his father did. Bob tightened the grip on his shoulder before releasing him and said in a very level voice, "No problems whatsoever, Mr. Pye."

"I see." Mr. Pye scribbled busily on his clipboard, while Neil looked up uncertainly at his father, who remained silent and stone-faced.

Eventually Mr. Pye spoke again. "I'm bound to tell you, Mr. Parker, that I'm not satisfied. The insurance company can't pay you until we have identified the cause of the fire. I'll be sending some of my colleagues to take a closer examination on Monday. I would be grateful if the site remained untouched until we've made our report. Good day, Mr. Parker."

Mr. Pye retrieved his briefcase, put his clipboard away, and stalked off toward the gate. Bob watched him go, declining to escort him to the car.

"I wonder," Bob muttered under his breath. "Did I leave something in there? I keep trying to think . . ."

Neil heard him and said, "You couldn't have, Dad. You're so careful about things like that."

Bob shrugged. "The police were back this morning. They were poking around for hours. I suppose they think it was my fault, too."

Neil didn't like the worried tone of his father's voice. "Dad, what did Mr. Pye mean? About being in debt?"

Bob looked down. Neil was shocked at the spark of fury in his eyes. His dad hardly ever got angry. "I think Mr. Pye believes I caused the fire myself to get the insurance money."

"What!" Neil clenched his fists tightly in frustration and took a step toward the gate, but by now Mr. Pye had vanished.

Bob gave a short laugh, but not as if he thought anything was funny. "Going after him won't solve anything, Neil." He let out a sigh. "But if the insurance company doesn't pay up, we won't be able to rebuild the barn. And if they, or the police, say I'm negligent, the council won't renew my license. The kennel might not be able to carry on."

Neil looked at his father anxiously as he saw his shoulders sag.

Bob put his hands in his pockets and kicked at a lump of burned wood. "Well, what does it matter? Maybe there's no point in carrying on anyway."

CHAPTER FOUR

Neil and Emily were worried about their father. Bob Parker was the most cheerful, even-tempered person they knew. He was never depressed, he was rarely angry, and he cared passionately about King Street Kennels and all the dogs who came there. How could he even think of giving all that up? The idea that their dad could even consider it really bothered them.

Bob hardly spoke during lunch. His silence affected the mood of everyone at the table, and it was one of the most miserable meals Neil could ever remember having at home. He wanted to talk in a whisper, but ended up not talking at all.

As they were clearing their plates at the end of the meal, the phone rang in the hallway. Carole went to answer it and came back looking more cheerful. "That was Mike Turner," she announced. "He's got Red in the intensive care unit and says that he's stabilized a little. His injuries are still very severe, but Mike thinks there's a chance he'll pull through."

"A chance is better than nothing," said Emily, managing to smile. "He's holding on. He's surviving."

"Red will have to stay there for some time, of course," Carole continued. "But Brownie's fine and we can pick him up anytime we like."

Bob Parker grunted. "You'd better go now," he said quietly. "Jim Birchall's funeral is at four, and I'll want the Range Rover when you get back."

"But, Dad," Neil protested, "don't you want to come and see Red?"

Bob gave him an uneasy look, almost as if he felt guilty about something. This worried Neil even more. Was his father blaming himself because Red got hurt?

"Not right now," Bob said. "I've got things to do."

Neil and Emily accompanied their mother to Mike Turner's office and grew more anxious about seeing Red as they got closer to Compton.

Janice, the vet's receptionist and nurse, greeted them as they entered through the main doors. "Mike's with a patient," she said. "A cat with an eye infection. He'll be with you in a few minutes. Do you want to go straight through to the intensive care unit?"

Neil had visited the intensive care unit at the animal hospital once or twice before, but seeing it again still filled him with a sense of dread. It meant that a dog had been seriously injured, and to Neil that was the worst thing that could happen. The ICU was how Neil imagined a hospital operating room would be; everything was white or shiny, and there was a strong smell of disinfectant.

Animals were housed in separate heated cages and a notice on each cage gave details of their injuries and treatment to date. The whole area was kept clean and quiet, and Mike gave them all the best treatment there was. Despite this, Neil still found it a depressing place.

Red was the only patient in the unit. He was asleep in his cage on a heated pad. Neil thought he was dead at first, but then he saw the faint rise and fall of the dog's body as he breathed. An intravenous drip was taped to Red's left foreleg and his broken back leg was in a plaster cast. A section of his coat over his stomach had been shaved away and a white dressing was taped over the bare patch.

"What happened there?" Neil asked aloud.

Footsteps sounded behind them as Mike Turner came into the room. "A large splinter from the piece of wood that struck him inflicted a deep wound to his stomach. His internal injuries were serious enough to make me operate immediately. He's had several stitches, but . . ."

"Will he pull through?" asked Emily anxiously.

"I don't know," Mike replied. He shook his head, hesitated for a minute, and then added more briskly, "He was cold and he'd lost blood. But he's a strong dog and he's been well looked after. There was no spinal damage, but I'll be honest with you, it could still go either way."

Neil and Emily gazed into Red's cage, while their mother studied the notes fastened to the cage.

"Come on, boy," Neil said. "You can get better — you've got to." *You've got to, for Dad,* he added silently to himself.

"And what about Brownie?" Carole asked.

"Ah, well." Mike rubbed his chin thoughtfully. "You've got a different sort of problem there. There's nothing physically wrong with him, but . . . come and look."

Neil, Emily, and Carole followed Mike out to the back of the hospital where Mike had a couple of small pens for animals waiting until their owners picked them up. Brownie was in the first pen they came to, cowering in the back corner and looking terrified.

"He's been twitching ever since he arrived," Carole said. "And I don't suppose the fire has done him any good. I'll go and get the pet carrier."

Neil wasn't surprised that it took a few minutes to persuade Brownie into the pet carrier. Even Emily's coaxing didn't help much. The little brown dog kept drawing back his lips, snarling at anyone who wanted to touch him. Neil knew that he wasn't a savage dog. He was just frightened and trying to defend himself. But it would be impossible to find him a new owner until he learned to trust people again.

As Carole was turning the Range Rover into the driveway at King Street, Bob Parker opened the gate that led to the kennels. He looked unfamiliar, dressed for the funeral in a dark suit with a white shirt and a black tie.

A woman followed Bob, leading a fox terrier that Neil recognized as one of the current boarding dogs. As Neil and Emily jumped out of the Range Rover, they heard her launch into a verbal attack on their father.

"I couldn't believe it when I heard! The whole place could have burned to the ground. You're not fit to take care of my dog, Mr. Parker!" She dragged her dog over to her car, got in, and before slamming the door behind her said, "And I'm going to tell all my friends about King Street, believe me." The woman drove off with a spray of gravel from the wheels of her car.

Bob Parker rubbed the back of his neck. "Well, that's one dog we won't see again. At least she wasn't a regular."

Neil couldn't believe the woman's extreme reaction.

"What nerve," gasped Emily.

"Red's had an operation, Dad," said Neil, trying to cheer up his father. "Mike said it went really well. His spine isn't hurt, and Mike says he's strong and might pull through. And we've brought Brownie back. I want to —"

"Neil, I'm sorry, but I don't have time for that now," his father said roughly. "I've got a funeral to go to." He got behind the wheel of the Range Rover as Carole got out. "I'll be back for dinner," he said. Carole barely had time to get Brownie's pet carrier before he started up the car again and drove away.

Carole disappeared into the house, and Neil and Emily stood gazing at the open gate.

"That's not like Dad," Emily said.

"I know. Em, has he said anything else to you about giving up the kennel?" Emily shook her head and said nothing. "I told you how upset he was when the guy from the insurance company was here, didn't I? I can't believe they'd suspect him of burning down his own barn for the insurance money. And if people are starting to take their dogs away . . ." Neil's voice wavered, and he shrugged. "Come on, let's find some-place to put Brownie."

As Neil and Emily went through the gate into the courtyard, they met Kate McGuire coming out of Kennel Block Two. As always, she seemed to brighten up the place. Today she was wearing an orange scarf tied around her long, blond hair, and a brightly striped, baggy sweater.

"You've got Brownie," she said, coming up to Neil and Emily. "He can go back into the rescue center. I'll take him, if you like."

"He's a little nervous," Neil warned her.

"Can we do anything to help you out?" Emily asked.

"Please," Kate said. "I haven't been able to exercise all the dogs yet. If you could take a few out, that would be great."

"Sure," Neil said. "We'll tell Mom that we'll be out for a while."

They left Brownie with Kate and went back to the house. They found Carole in the office, switching on the computer.

"Fine," she said when Neil told her what they wanted to do. "That'll give me a chance to catch up on some of the paperwork."

Neil hesitated, then asked, "Mom, has Dad been talking about giving up the kennel?"

Carole looked directly at them both and sighed. "Your dad's upset. The fire is a serious matter, and the insurance claim has to go through, otherwise we can't afford to rebuild. His friend has just died, too, and I think Red being in such bad shape is upsetting him even more." She tried to smile. "Just give him some space, OK?"

"But, Mom," said Emily, "you won't really let Dad give up, will you?"

"Don't worry, we'll talk it all over before anybody decides anything. But just think about one thing, both of you — this is a very tough job. Nobody can do it if their heart isn't in it."

Bob Parker hadn't returned to King Street by the time Carole had prepared dinner. She held back serving the meal until Sarah began to fidget and became impatient. It was almost her bedtime.

"I'm serving dinner!" Carole decided and called down the hall for Neil and Emily to come to the table.

As Neil took his place, he suspected that she was trying to hide how worried she really was about his father. She busied herself in a whirlwind of activity getting everybody seated and the food prepared. "I'll keep your father's meal in the oven. I'm sure he won't be long."

Everyone had just taken their first mouthfuls when Bob Parker appeared at the back door. Neil thought he looked more tired now than he had after the fire. He crossed the room and sat down heavily. He rubbed his hands over his face slowly and silently.

"I'm sorry I'm late," Bob said at last, sounding as if he was forcing out the words. "I had to stay to hear about Jim's will. He left me something."

Neil wanted to ask what. He couldn't help thinking that it might be enough money to rebuild the barn. Maybe that would encourage his father to carry on, and everything would return to normal. But he said nothing. Bob already knew what his legacy was and he didn't look encouraged.

"What did he leave you, Bob?" Carole asked quietly.

"Red. He left me Red."

Neil caught his breath and saw how shocked Emily looked, too. They both knew how much that would have meant to their father the day before. But now? After what had happened?

"Jim knew I cared a lot about Red," Bob continued. "He even left me some money for his keep." He sighed and rubbed his hands across his face again. "I don't suppose he thought I would let him down so badly before he was even buried."

"You didn't!" Emily protested. "You can't —"

"Let's not talk about it, OK?"

Neil put his head down and concentrated on finishing his meal. He was relieved to escape the stony silence and leave his plate half-empty to go and answer the doorbell when it rang.

The man was no one he recognized. He was a smallish man, a bit overweight, with thinning dark hair. He wore green boots and expensive tweeds over a yellow vest.

"Hello, young man," he said. Neil didn't like his forced, jovial voice or being called "young man." "Can I have a word with your father?"

"I'm sorry," Neil replied frostily. "The kennel is closed until tomorrow morning."

"Ah, but this isn't kennel business," the man said, slightly annoyed. "So please call your father for me, kiddo."

Neil liked being called "kiddo" even less. He turned and yelled down the hallway for his father and after a moment Bob Parker came to the door.

"Yes?"

The stranger took Bob's hand and shook it vigorously. Neil hovered close by, curious to know who the visitor was. He exchanged a glance with Emily, who had appeared from the kitchen, and shrugged as she looked at him questioningly.

"Good evening, Mr. Parker," the caller said. "Or may I call you Bob? We haven't met, but I've seen you around. My name's Philip Kendall. I recently took over Old Mill Farm. My land shares a border with yours."

Bob nodded. "Oh, yes." He sounded vague, as if he was not really taking in what was being said to him. "I remember hearing about you, Mr. Kendall. What can I do for you?"

Philip Kendall smiled, and Neil instinctively thought it looked fake.

"It's more of a question of what *I* can do for *you*. I heard you had some trouble last night, Bob, and I have a proposition to put to you. Do you think I could come in and discuss it?"

"I'm sorry, Mr. Kendall, it's really not convenient at the moment."

"Nonsense, man," Kendall snapped. "Any time's convenient for business. That's how to succeed. I want to make you an offer." When Bob still did not reply or look interested, he added sharply, "I want to buy this place. And I'm prepared to give you a good price for it."

CHAPTER FIVE

Bob Parker remained silent for a moment, lost in thought. Philip Kendall's offer to buy King Street Kennels had taken him completely by surprise.

Neil stared wide-eyed at his sister, shocked at what the man had just said.

"You'd better come into the office," Bob said calmly, stepping outside. "It's this way." Kendall smiled and the two men disappeared in the direction of the kennel's office around the side of the house. Neil heard the door close behind them.

"Neil! Come and finish your dinner." His mother's voice echoed down the hallway.

Neil went back into the kitchen and sat down. Emily picked up her fork again, looking pale and miserable. The only noise came from Sarah, who was chattering happily about her ballet class the following day.

"Bedtime, Sarah," said Carole suddenly. Without giving her time to argue, Carole picked her up from her chair and whisked her upstairs.

"'Night, Neil. 'Night, Emily," echoed down the stairs and into the kitchen.

Neil forked down the remains of his cold meal without really tasting it. He couldn't imagine that his father would even think about selling King Street Kennels. He had assumed that they would always live there. He had assumed that he would join his dad in the business when he finished school. It seemed he had assumed many things that were now suddenly in danger of not happening at all.

"I don't want Dad to sell to that horrible man," Emily muttered. "He's not even a real farmer."

"How can you tell?"

"He's dressed how he thinks a farmer should dress," Emily said. "He doesn't *know*. And there's no mud on his boots. He hasn't been near a muddy field in his life!"

Neil would have laughed if he hadn't been so worried. Emily was right.

"Dad won't sell," he said, trying to sound reassuring. "Not to him. Not to anybody. Where would we go?"

Emily shrugged and didn't answer.

Neil put down his fork and scraped what was left on his plate into a bowl on the floor for Sam to polish off. While they were clearing the table, they heard Carole come downstairs and go into the office.

"Mom won't let Dad sell," he said. He wished he believed it, but he suddenly wasn't so sure.

Emily started running water into the sink and squirted in dish-washing soap. After watching her for a minute Neil got a towel. Washing up was better than doing nothing but worrying.

"You know," Emily said, "it's funny."

"What's funny?" That was the last word Neil would have used to describe life just now.

"Why would that man come and offer to buy the kennel now? Just after the barn's burned down. When Dad's . . . not himself."

Neil stood with a glass in his hand, staring at her. He was starting to catch on. It was a strange coincidence. No one had ever suggested buying the kennel before. "Well . . ." he said feebly. "Maybe he had always planned to make Dad an offer."

"And maybe he knows more than he's telling." Emily scrubbed a plate viciously with the scrub brush. "He was on our doorstep pretty quick, wasn't he? Maybe he burned down the barn himself!"

"Oh, come on, Em . . ."

"Nobody knows how the fire started," Emily pointed out. "You told me that insurance man wasn't satisfied. He even thought *Dad* did it!"

Neil went on drying dishes. There was something in what Emily said. He found it hard to think of would-be farmer Philip Kendall as a criminal, but it was strange that his offer had come just now — at the one time when Neil's dad was likely to listen to him. Maybe it was more than coincidence. At the very least, Kendall might be trying to get the kennel cheap because they were having trouble. "We could never prove he started it," he said.

"We can try," said Emily. "If there's even the smallest possibility that Dad might sell to him, we'll have to try."

Minutes later, Neil and Emily heard the office door open and the front door open and close. Not long after that, slow footsteps could be heard going upstairs, and their mother came back into the kitchen.

"Oh, thank you," she said warmly, noticing that they had cleared the table and done the washing up. "That's a real help." Usually so full of energy, Carole suddenly looked tired, and when she sat down at the kitchen table she sighed and shook her head.

"Cup of tea, Mom?" Emily suggested.

"Please." Carole managed to smile. "It's been a long day."

Emily put the kettle on the stove.

"Where's Dad?" asked Neil. "What's happening? Is he going to sell? Where will we —"

Carole put up a hand to stop the flood of questions. "Your dad's gone to bed. He's been up longer than any of us. But there's no need to panic. Nothing has been decided."

"But he's listening to that man," Emily groaned. "Before all this happened, he would have just told him to go away."

"Why does Mr. Kendall want the kennel anyway?" Neil asked. "He's got a farm of his own."

"He wants to extend his land and have better access to Compton Road. I think he wants to put one of his managers into the house. Mr. Kendall doesn't work the farm himself — other people do that for him."

"But, Mom! We can't leave the house!"

Emily gave Neil a nod, as if she wanted to say, *I was right about Mr. Kendall!*

"I don't want strangers in our house," Neil said. "This is our place. Besides, what would Dad do if he sold the kennel?"

"I don't know." Carole smiled at Emily as she put the cup of tea in front of her. "Thanks, love." She sipped the tea and let out a long sigh. "I told you, there's a lot to talk about yet. Nothing will happen quickly. Give your father a few days to get over the shock. He might see things differently then."

Or he might not, Neil thought quietly to himself.

The next day was Saturday. Carole took Sarah off to her ballet class, and Neil and Emily helped Kate McGuire with the morning feeding and exercising of the dogs.

Bob Parker didn't come down for breakfast.

When they had brought the last of the boarding dogs back after their morning walks, Kate turned to Neil and Emily and announced that she felt sorry for Brownie. "He needs somebody to love him, I think. Let's see what we can do for him. It might cheer your father up a bit if we can get the pooch smiling again."

Neil and Emily welcomed the distraction and headed for the rescue center. They walked with her past the blackened remains of the barn. Sections of it were fenced off with bright orange tape and other parts were covered with plastic sheeting.

Brownie was still cowering in the corner of his pen. He had hardly touched the bowl of food Kate had given him earlier. Kate took the leash down from its hook outside the pen. "Let me deal with him. Your mom and dad won't be too pleased if I let you get bitten."

"He's not dangerous," Emily protested. "Just frightened, the poor thing."

"And that means he's likely to bite if he feels cornered," Kate said. She went into the pen and spoke soothingly to the little mutt. Brownie growled at first, his lips drawn back and his tail between his legs. But at last he settled down enough for Kate to clip on the leash. He was still not keen to leave the safety of his pen, and he pulled back when Kate tried to coax him out.

"Why don't you bring Blackie?" she suggested to Neil. "That should give Brownie the right idea. Not even Brownie could be scared of Blackie!"

Before she had finished speaking, Emily was already opening the door of Blackie's pen. The puppy bounced up to her and scrambled to cover her face with wet licks as she squatted down to clip on the leash.

"Get off!" Emily spluttered. "Silly dog!"

Blackie immediately misunderstood and rolled onto her back with her paws in the air, waiting to have her stomach tickled.

"She could use a little training, too," Neil said, grinning as he watched them.

Neil, Emily, and Kate set off toward the exercise field. Both dogs were pulling on their leashes, with Blackie eager to get where they were going the quickest and Brownie wanting to go back to the shelter of his pen. Neil whistled for Sam, who came bounding up to him but walked correctly at heel

when Neil put on his leash. Somebody had to show these dogs the proper way to behave.

In the exercise field, Emily concentrated on getting Blackie to walk to heel. It proved difficult because the little black puppy was too interested in what was going on around her and kept wanting to run off and sniff some fascinating new smell or chase her own tail. Neil offered a word of advice now and again, while Sam tolerated Blackie's antics.

Neil's thoughts drifted toward Red lying alone and barely clinging to life in Mike Turner's animal hospital. Neil promised himself that he would call the vet as soon as he had finished with the dogs in the field.

Kate wasn't having much success with Brownie. The brown mutt crouched in the grass and shivered, not responding to any of Kate's commands. Even getting him to stand was nearly impossible. Neil's suggestions and attempts to persuade him didn't work, either. *Both dogs,* Neil thought, *could do with his father's obedience classes.*

Then another thought occurred to him. "What's going to happen to the obedience classes, now that the barn's burned down?" he asked.

"I don't know," Kate replied. "Your dad hasn't said anything to me."

Neil exchanged glances with Emily. There was quite a lot Kate still didn't know, and Neil felt slightly uncomfortable keeping secrets from one of his best friends.

"The next scheduled class is tomorrow morning," Emily said. "I suppose we could have it out here, if the weather's good."

Neil didn't reply. Of course Emily was right. But there wasn't just the problem of where to hold the classes. He couldn't help wondering if his father would want to hold them at all.

When Blackie had walked off some of her friskiness, Emily tried teaching her to sit. She didn't get very far. Blackie thought she would much rather lie on her back with her paws waving or roll in the grass. When at last she sat on command — and Neil thought it might have been just because she felt like sitting — Emily fussed over her and told her what a brilliant dog she was. The puppy loved the attention.

"Stop there," Kate said. "Always finish the session when the dog's done something right. That way she'll want to learn next time."

Neil wished that they could do the same for Brownie, but the nervous little dog wasn't responding at all. He and Kate tried again, this time with the stay and recall commands. There was no problem in getting Brownie to stay, but he didn't want to come to either of them when they called him.

Eventually Kate ended the training session.

"That's enough for now," she said. "I don't think we'll get any further today."

They led the dogs back to the rescue center. Emily had made some progress in persuading Blackie to scamper beside her, but Brownie still pulled against the leash and didn't want to go anywhere near Kate.

As they rounded the corner of Kennel Block Two, Neil saw his father standing with his hands in his pockets and staring moodily at the ruins of the barn. He looked unhappy, but at least it was a relief to see him outside and in his old corduroys and green King Street Kennels sweatshirt. His dark funeral suit and black tie had made him look so different.

"Dad," Emily said, remembering their last conversation in the field as they approached him. "What about the obedience class tomorrow? Will you have it in the field? Can I bring Blackie?"

Bob didn't look at her. "There won't be a class tomorrow," he said. His eyes had a glazed look about them. "I asked your mother to call and tell everybody that the classes have been canceled until further notice."

Nobody responded.

Neil didn't dare ask his father if the classes had been abandoned forever.

"I could do with some help with Brownie, Bob," Kate said, breaking the silence. "The poor little thing just sits there trembling. I'm not sure anybody's going to want him like this."

Bob turned around and stared down for a minute at the cowering dog. "If that dog hadn't run off into the barn," he said slowly, "Red would never have been hurt." He watched Brownie for a minute longer and then, without another word, turned back toward the house.

Neil stared after him. A dark, hollow fear was opening up inside him. He had never seen his father literally turn his back on a dog who needed him.

CHAPTER SIX

"Neil! What are you doing?" Emily walked up to her brother later that afternoon and pulled him away from the office windows.

Neil put a finger to his lips and asked her to be quiet. "I'm listening to Mom and Dad. I was going to call Mike Turner from the phone in the office, when I heard them discussing what they're going to do," he whispered. Cocking his ear toward the office, he resumed eavesdropping on his parents.

"Why didn't you say so?" Emily said. "Move over and let me listen, too." She crept up beside him and took up the same stance with total curiosity.

Their parents were in the office having a heated discussion.

"This is our home, Bob," they heard their mother

say. "The children are in a good school and the disruption would be terrible for them."

"He's offering a good price, Carole," Bob replied. "I'm just saying maybe we should think about it seriously."

"And then what? If we sell King Street, *how* are we going to live and *where* are we going to live?"

"We can get jobs. We've both been employed before."

Neil could imagine the look of exasperation on his mother's face.

"After being your own boss? Bob, you'd hate it. You know you would."

"I'm not so sure, Carole. . . ." Their father sounded tired and discouraged. "Maybe I'm just not up to this work anymore. Look at what's happened this week."

"That's not true and you know it!"

In spite of his anxiety, Neil grinned. At least his mother was putting up a fight!

"You're needed here in Compton, Bob. There's nobody else around here who does what we do. We can't just give up and walk away."

"That's all very well, but if the insurance company won't honor my claim, and if the council won't renew my license to work on the premises next year, I'm finished anyway."

His father sounded so hopeless that suddenly Neil didn't want to go on listening. He turned away from the office door and almost ran to the kitchen. Emily

followed him more slowly. While Neil helped himself
to a chocolate-chip cookie and a glass of milk, Emily
grabbed a pencil and some paper and sat down at
the table, chewing the end of her pencil, deep in
thought.

"What are you doing?" Neil asked.

Emily looked up. "I think we should figure out how
to raise some money. If they won't give Dad the insurance money, maybe we can rebuild the barn our-
selves." She leaned over the paper again and started
to write. "We could have a yard sale, and maybe get
sponsored to do something, or walk other people's
dogs. . . ."

"No, that's pointless," Neil said. "We'd never make
enough. Chris Wilson's dad had a new garage built
last year and he said it cost him nearly three
months' wages. A small fortune — just for a garage!
How much do you think it would cost to build a barn
that's three times the size? Get real, Em!"

Emily flushed and tears sprang to her eyes. She
crumpled up the piece of paper and hurled it across
the kitchen. "At least I'm trying to think of something!"

"I'm sorry," Neil said. "But honestly . . ."

Sam padded across the kitchen and nosed at the
ball of paper. Then he picked it up in his mouth and
brought it back to Emily, eager to join in this new
game.

Emily suddenly started to laugh. "OK, so that was

silly," she said. "But there must be *something* we can do."

Neil crunched his cookie and thought.

"We'll never earn enough for the barn," he said, "not with school and everything we do here. There'd never be enough time in a million years. But maybe people would donate things.... Remember what Mom said: 'They need us here in Compton.'"

"True."

"Just think of everyone Mom and Dad have helped in the past. Maybe they'd help us, now that we need it."

Emily was smiling again and her eyes were shining. She grabbed her pencil and another piece of paper. "Who should we ask?"

Neil and Emily's list was almost two pages long when their mother came back into the kitchen. Emily was so busy scribbling down names that she didn't notice Carole arrive.

"We can get Jake Fielding to write something about us in the *Compton News*," Emily blurted out. "He's bound to want to cover the story of the fire, and we can pull his heartstrings about all the poor dogs that need help. I'll call him now!"

"Whoa! Hold on!" said Carole as Emily pushed back her chair and almost bumped into her mother.

"Sorry, Mom!" Emily apologized. "But I'm on a mission."

"I heard. Unfortunately, you've already missed him," Carole said.

"Eh?" said Neil incredulously. "How come?"

"Jake was here yesterday morning, while you two were still in bed. He got the story and took plenty of photographs. It'll be in the *Compton News* next Friday in all its lurid detail."

"But we want him to ask people to help us," Emily said.

Carole frowned. "What are you two plotting?"

Emily explained their plan to get the friends of King Street Kennels to rally for them.

"Well . . ." Carole looked uncertain. "I won't have you asking for money. That's enough of that. In any case, it's not money that's our main problem."

No, Neil thought. *It's Dad.*

Emily looked as if she might throw the second piece of paper across the kitchen, too. "We're only trying to help!"

"I know. Don't think I'm not grateful. But . . . just tell people what happened, OK? What they do about it is up to them."

In the early evening, Neil and Emily rode their bikes into Compton to see Red for the first time in twenty-four hours. They were desperately hoping that there had been some improvement in his condition over the weekend and arrived at Mike Turner's animal hospital full of high hopes and expectations.

Although there were no official office hours on Saturday, Mike was there anyway catching up on paperwork. He took Neil and Emily into the intensive care unit. Red was still lying on the mat in his cage and still had the IV drip attached to his leg.

"Isn't he getting better at all?" Emily asked anxiously.

"He's stable," said Mike. "It's early yet. But he is a little stronger."

Looking at the dog closely, Neil thought he could detect a difference. Last time they had seen the Irish setter, he had looked as if he were dead. Now Neil could see that Red's breathing was much steadier and stronger and, though his eyes were closed, it was more like ordinary sleep.

"He's a determined fella," Mike said. "I thought he would be. Irish setters were bred to be hunting dogs, you know — out every day in all kinds of weather. He's not some spoiled little lapdog. He's tough."

"Can we touch him?" Emily asked.

Mike Turner nodded and opened the door of the cage. Emily reached in and gently stroked the setter's head. Red's eyes opened, he turned his head a little, and gave her hand a feeble lick.

"Hey, great!" Neil said. He reached carefully into the cage and gave Red a pat. The setter whined softly, closed his eyes again, and settled back into sleep.

Mike Turner grinned. "Don't think all his troubles are over yet. There's still a long way to go."

"Mike," Neil began while they stood looking at the peaceful dog. "Dad's really upset about all this. . . ." Neil explained about the insurance claim and Philip Kendall's offer to buy the kennel.

"That's why Red *has* to get better," added Emily when her brother had finished.

"And you want to drum up some support?" Mike said. "Well, count me in. Plenty of your father's clients come through here and I'll talk to anybody I think might be prepared to help. I'll let you know what people think they can do."

"Thanks!" Neil said.

Emily took her list of names out of her pocket and checked off Mike's name.

Mike laughed. "You'll be all right now, Neil," he said, looking at Emily. "You've got your chief public relations officer on the job!"

Despite the evening chill, Neil felt as though the sun had come out as they left Red in the ICU and stepped outside. In spite of the vet's cautious diagnosis, Neil was convinced that Red was going to be all right. And everything else would be all right, too. It had to be.

CHAPTER SEVEN

After school on Monday, Neil met Emily in the playground. They had planned some stops on their way back to King Street and told their mother that they would be home late.

"What a hectic day!" said Neil, pretending to wipe his brow. "Everybody has heard about the fire. I think I was the most popular kid in school today."

"You, too, huh?" said Emily. "Enjoy your fame while it lasts, Neil Parker. You'll be the weird dog-kid again by the end of the week."

Neil laughed. "You're totally right there. But lots of people said they'd help out if we needed it. Hasheem and some of the others offered to help us rebuild the barn."

"Yeah? That's great. But let's reel in some of the

bigger fish first, shall we? Who's at the top of the list?"

"Well, Mrs. Smedley from the general store is top — but Marjorie Foster's closest. She should still be in her office if we go right away," Neil suggested.

"OK! Let's go!"

Marjorie Foster worked for a local law firm called White and Marbeck. Her father had nearly lost his beautiful collie earlier that year when the dog had been wrongly accused of attacking sheep. Neil and Emily had worked hard to reunite Skye with the old man, who was now living in a residential home, and they thought his daughter owed them a big favor.

White and Marbeck's offices were in Compton's Market Square. Neil and Emily climbed the narrow, dusty stairs to the top floor and spoke to the receptionist. The receptionist spoke into an intercom and then took them down a hallway that led to a large, spacious room. It was decorated with huge bookcases and wood paneling and it looked more like an ornate living room than an office.

Marjorie Foster was a middle-aged woman with neatly styled brown hair. She was tall, slim, and wore a stylish blue suit.

"Hello," she said when Neil and Emily entered the room. She closed a huge leather-bound book and sat down. "I haven't seen you two for a while. What can I do for you?" She waved Neil and Emily to chairs opposite her desk.

Emily quickly recounted to her the events at King Street Kennels since the terrifying early hours of Friday morning. Mrs. Foster listened carefully and seemed genuinely touched by Neil's and Emily's concern for both Red and the fate of the kennel. She scribbled a quick note when Emily mentioned the name of Philip Kendall and returned to this point when Emily had finished her story.

"Why did Mr. Kendall say he wanted to buy the kennel?" Mrs. Foster asked, frowning.

"Mom said it was to farm the land and let one of his managers live in the house. *Our* house," said Neil indignantly.

Marjorie Foster was thinking. "Hmm. Very interesting. Very interesting indeed." Then she sat back in her chair and studied Neil and Emily closely. "White and Marbeck often deals with legal issues regarding land and planned changes of use. Sometimes, despite my position here, I don't agree with such changes. If you've got time, I'd like to tell you a little story."

Neil exchanged a glance with Emily.

"There was once a very rich man," began Marjorie Foster.

Neil was confused. Did Mrs. Foster think they were little kids who had to be entertained with fairy tales?

"The rich man wanted to become even richer," Mrs. Foster continued. "And he bought a farm just outside a little country town —"

"Like Compton?" Emily interrupted. She was beginning to catch on to what Mrs. Foster was trying to tell them.

"Yes, someplace like Compton. But the rich man didn't really want to farm the land. He wanted to sell it again, for a big profit, to another rich man who made his money by building supermarkets. They both thought that a shopping complex was just what this little country town needed."

"No way!" Neil said, speaking louder than he meant to.

"They submitted their plans to the local council," Marjorie Foster went on. "But the council refused planning permission. They may have decided that this was a good idea but the farm he was trying to sell wasn't close enough to the main road. And there wasn't enough space in the plans for a parking lot. That made the rich man very angry, because now he couldn't sell the farm and make his huge profit. The story ends with the man thinking he might be able to buy another small property just next door to his farm —"

"You mean King Street Kennels!" Neil couldn't help interrupting again. He couldn't remember when he had last been so furious. "And the rich man is Philip Kendall, isn't it?"

Mrs. Foster's face didn't react. "I didn't say that, Neil. I —"

"He wants to buy our land and build a supermarket!" Emily had turned red with anger. "And a parking lot!"

"He can't do that. Come on, Em, we've got to talk to Mom and Dad about this." Neil got up. "Thanks for telling us, Mrs. Foster."

Marjorie Foster looked up at him, her chin resting on her hands.

"I'm a lawyer, Neil. Confidentiality is my business. Remember this — I haven't told you anything today, except a story. I haven't mentioned any names."

"Got it!" Neil was grinning. "Thanks anyway. 'Bye!"

As he and Emily left the office, Marjorie Foster opened her book again with what looked like a smile of satisfaction on her face.

Neil and Emily arrived at King Street to discover their mother and father counting inventory in the storeroom between the two kennel blocks. Bob was sitting at the table, calling out items from a list on a clipboard, while Carole checked the shelves.

"Mom! Dad!" Neil said breathlessly. "You've got to listen to this."

"That's right!" said Emily. "You can stop adding everything up to see what it's worth!"

"Neil, Emily. We're not doing that. We perform inventory checks every week. You both know that. Look, this isn't more trouble, is it?" asked Carole. "This morning we had the insurance people crawling all over the barn, trying to find out how the fire

started. This afternoon we had another group from
the council doing the same thing and inspecting the
whole place for fire safety violations. Two people
have called to cancel their bookings. I don't think I
want to hear anything else tonight."

"You'll want to hear this," Neil said confidently.
"Philip Kendall's going to tear down the kennels and
build a supermarket."

"And a parking lot!" Emily added.

With Neil and Emily both trying to tell the story
at once, and with Bob and Carole trying to ask questions, it was a long time before everything was clear.

"Let's get this straight," Bob said at last. Neil
thought he was looking more alert, more like the dad
he knew. "Philip Kendall wants to sell his land to a
developer for a shopping complex. And the council
wouldn't take it any further at this stage because
the plans didn't have good enough access to the main
road?"

"That's right," Carole said. "The road down to Old
Mill Farm winds all over the place."

"There isn't room for a parking lot, either," Bob finished. "So Kendall makes an offer for this place,
meaning to pull everything down, put an entrance
road right through the middle of it, and lay down
concrete for his parking lot."

"That's not what he told us," Carole said.

Bob looked at them with a fierce grin. "Well, he

wouldn't, would he?" He stood up. "I'm going to find out more about this."

"How?" Neil asked.

"I'm going to call Councilman Jepson. He's been quite friendly ever since we helped him train those horrendous Westies of his. He should be able to tell me a little bit more about the subject of planning permission. . . ." He strode off toward the office.

Neil felt his spirits lifting. Maybe his dad was returning to his usual self. Maybe Bob Parker wanted to fight for King Street Kennels after all. Neil looked out at the courtyard and the kennel blocks and tried to picture the buildings torn down and everything covered with paved roads and lines of cars. Maybe

they would build a gas station on the exercise field where the dogs loved to run and play. The burned remains of the barn already made the view outside look completely different. "Dad won't let them flatten King Street, will he?"

"You bet he won't," his mom said confidently. "I've seen these suburban supermarkets before. They ruin the countryside. Everybody drives to them and that causes even more pollution on the roads."

"I bet it was Mr. Kendall who set fire to the barn!" cried Emily.

"I hope you haven't said that to anyone else," Carole said quickly.

"No, Mom, I'm not stupid. But it's a big coincidence, isn't it? The barn burns down just when Mr. Kendall wants to buy this place. It must have been him."

"We'll worry about what caused the fire later."

Neil couldn't help wondering if Emily was right, but his thoughts were interrupted by his father coming back from the office. Neil thought there was a strange look on his father's face. "What's happened?" he asked.

Everybody was looking at Bob.

"I called Mr. Jepson," he said. "And it's true — about the planning permission. The developer wanted to build a supermarket, gas station, a concourse for smaller shops, and a children's play area. The council rejected the first application for the reasons you had mentioned."

"But there's something else, isn't there?" Carole could sense it.

"Yes. I'd just put the phone down when it rang again. It was Paul Hamley from Meadowbank School. He said he'd heard Neil telling everybody about our situation in school today, and he asked if he could help in any way. Then he said that if we couldn't afford to rebuild, he would see the head principal about getting the whole school involved in a fund-raising project." Bob sounded as if he didn't quite believe what he was saying. He groped for a chair and sat down. "I don't know what to say. It's really amazing. The kindness of some people."

"It's no more than you deserve," said Carole.

Neil said nothing. He had never expected his teacher to be so nice!

On Tuesday afternoon, Neil and Emily were surprised to see their father waiting for them in the green Range Rover outside the school. Bob Parker still looked tired, but Neil thought he could see a new sparkle in his father's eyes.

"Hi, there," Bob said. "I'm going to see Red. Want to come with me?"

Neil grinned widely. One of the things that had worried him most was that Bob hadn't wanted to visit Red. It was a relief to see his father taking an interest in dogs again. Maybe now Neil would be able to enlist his father's help for Brownie, too.

Neil and Emily scrambled into the Range Rover. As usual, Sarah was late coming out of school and they waited patiently for her to arrive.

"Did anything happen today, Dad?" Neil asked tentatively.

"Well," Bob said. "The German shepherd's owner turned up and took him away. He was really pleased and made a donation to the rescue center. Apparently, he'd been visiting his sister in Colshaw and the dog ran away when he let him out of the car for a run."

"You'd think he'd put a tag on his collar with his phone number, wouldn't you?" Emily said.

"It's amazing how many people forget the obvious things."

"I'm not sorry to see the dog go," said Neil, crossing his arms. "He was too much of a handful."

"I got a call from one of our regular suppliers today, too," Bob went on. "He'd heard about the fire and offered to replace all the bedding that we'd lost for the rescue center free of charge." Bob shook his head and sounded astonished. "I was really touched by his generosity."

"You won't sell, will you, Dad?" Emily asked.

Neil caught his breath and wondered whether his

sister had been a bit hasty in asking the question. It might not have been the right time to ask.

Bob hesitated and fiddled with the car keys in the ignition. "I don't know. I need to do some more thinking. A lot will depend on what the insurance people find."

"But, Dad —"

"Look, there's Squirt." Neil was relieved to have a reason to interrupt. He wanted to tell Emily that there was no point in pushing their father now. It was best to let him think things over in peace.

"I wrote about the fire in my class diary," said Sarah proudly as she climbed into the car. "And everybody asked me to tell them about it."

"Well done, Squirt," Neil said.

Bob Parker started the car and set off, with Sarah bouncing up and down with excitement when she found out they were going to see Red.

When they reached the animal hospital, Neil was

disappointed to find that Red was still in the intensive care unit. He'd been hoping that he might see the Irish setter up and around, closer to his lively, confident self. But at least the drip had been removed and he was awake. When the Parkers went in he lifted his head and barked — quite a weak bark — but it showed that he recognized them.

Bob opened the cage, patted him, and Red's tongue rasped across his hand.

"Can I pet him?" Sarah asked.

"Yes," Mike Turner said, "but be very gentle."

"Well, Mike," Bob said, biting his lip, "what's the verdict? Is he going to make it?"

Mike was looking serious. He spoke in a low voice so that Sarah, chatting happily to Red, couldn't hear what he said to the others. "He's coming along, but I can't be sure yet. It was a difficult operation to repair the internal wounds. A lot of dogs wouldn't have survived it. And there's always the chance of an infection — you often get that with stomach wounds. But if I was going to bet on any dog, I'd bet on Red. He's a fighter."

Bob looked across the room to where Sarah was still stroking the Irish setter. Neil could see how proud he was of the dog and how much he cared about him.

"He is," Bob said. "And he's got to fight now. We've all got to."

CHAPTER EIGHT

The Parkers' Range Rover followed a dirty white van up Compton Road on the way back from the vet. It had some lumber poking out of the back with a scrap of red rag tied to it. Neil and his father, in the front two seats, were surprised when the van turned into the drive of King Street Kennels.

"I wonder who that is," Neil said. "I don't recognize the van."

A middle-aged man in overalls jumped down from the van's driving seat. He had a receding hairline and a weather-beaten face. "Mr. Parker?" The man stuck out a hand as Bob climbed out of the Range Rover. "Eddie Thomas."

Bob shook hands with him, but he still looked bewildered.

"I'm Dave Thomas's brother," the man explained. "From the garage in Compton? You gave him and his wife a dog from your rescue center."

The expression on Bob's face cleared. "Yes, of course, Dave Thomas."

Neil remembered, too. Dave had saved a wonderful dog named Billy from being put to sleep when nobody else had offered him a home.

"What can I do for you, Mr. Thomas?" said Bob. "Are you looking for a dog for yourself?"

Eddie Thomas laughed. "Call me Eddie. No, I can't say I've ever thought about having a dog. It was always our Dave who liked them. It's because of him that I'm here now. He told me you were having some trouble."

Bob scratched his chin. "You could say that."

"Well, you see, I'm a builder by trade, and —"

"Now hang on a minute, Mr. Thomas — Eddie," Bob said. "I don't know that I can afford a builder just yet. The insurance might not pay up and I can't touch the site until they tell me they're finished with it."

"No problem," Eddie said. He took a crumpled envelope out of his pocket and a pencil from behind his ear. He licked the pencil point and started to scribble. "I can get you lumber at cost, and as for labor, well, we can sort that out later. Where's the barn?" He pointed to the gate at the side of the house. "This way? Let me take a look." He strode off toward the gate.

Bob looked at Neil and Emily, shrugged helplessly, and followed. Neil and Emily both started to laugh.

"That's telling him!" Neil said.

"Perhaps we really *will* get the barn rebuilt now," Emily added.

"How long has this one been here?" Eddie Thomas was peering into Blackie's pen in the rescue center after having finished estimating the cost of replacing the King Street Kennels barn.

"Only a couple of weeks," said Bob. Blackie bounced across to Eddie and put her paws up on the mesh, panting excitedly. "We'll have no trouble placing her, I expect. She's just the type young people go for."

Eddie walked a few paces farther along the row of pens and stopped in front of Brownie. "And this timid thing?"

"His name's Brownie," explained Neil. "He's been badly scared by something and he's still unsettled, so we don't think it'll be as easy finding him a new home."

Eddie sighed. "That's a shame."

Bob stood looking thoughtfully into Brownie's pen. Neil was glad to see his father beginning to take an interest in Brownie again. But when Eddie stepped back and started poking his finger through the mesh of Blackie's pen, he couldn't help wondering whether they had found a new owner for the puppy. "Would you like to have her, Mr. Thomas?"

Eddie Thomas straightened up, shaking his head. "No, I've never had a dog. I wouldn't know where to start and I'm too old to learn." He hesitated, and then added, "Mind you, the wife likes dogs. . . ."

"Why not ask her?" Neil suggested. "We won't let Blackie go until you decide."

"I don't know. . . ." Eddie shook his head again, but he looked back at Blackie as he left the rescue center. Bob and Neil exchanged sly grins behind his back.

As Carole Parker drove their car through the entrance to the kennels after school on Thursday, Neil and Emily noticed a shiny BMW parked in front of the house. Philip Kendall, still in his tweeds and clean boots, was about to get into it. He stopped when the Range Rover pulled up and Carole got out.

"Mrs. Parker?" he said, offering a handshake. "I just rang your doorbell but your husband doesn't seem to be at home."

Carole shook his hand but, by the strange grimace on his mother's face, Neil couldn't help thinking that she looked as if somebody had just offered her a dead rat. "He's probably around the back with the dogs," she said. "Do you want to go see him?"

Philip Kendall looked annoyed and shuffled his feet as though he expected her to get Bob for him. He followed her through the side gate. Neil and Emily followed him, but Sarah said, "Nasty man," loudly enough for Mr. Kendall to hear and ran back into the house.

Kate McGuire was sweeping the courtyard. Before Carole could ask her where Bob was, Sam came racing over from the direction of the exercise field and Neil saw his father returning from a walk with some of the boarding dogs. Emily went to help. She and Kate took the dogs inside, while Bob came over to where Philip Kendall was waiting.

"Now, look here, Mr. Parker," Kendall began as soon as Bob was in earshot. "This won't do. It's been almost a week since I made you my offer and I really can't wait any longer. I want an answer."

"I can't make a big decision like that in five minutes," Bob said coolly. "I need time to think."

Kendall gave a snort of disgust. "If you take much longer to decide, I might change my mind."

Neil tried to catch his father's eye. He wanted to see if Bob was going to confront Mr. Kendall with what he knew. He was itching to ask Kendall about it himself, but he knew his father would be furious if he interfered.

Neil snapped his fingers at Sam, who ran over and sat beside him, passing close to Philip Kendall as he did so. Kendall's foot twitched, as if he would have kicked the Border collie if nobody had been watching him. "Can't we discuss this in private?" the man asked.

"I don't think there's anything more to discuss," Bob said calmly.

"Ha!" Kendall sounded satisfied. "We're agreed, then. I'll get my lawyer to draw up a contract."

"I'm sorry, you've misunderstood me," Bob said. "If you insist on getting an answer this instant, then I'm turning down your offer."

Neil felt like cheering. He saw his mother smile as if she hadn't known what Bob was going to do until this moment.

"You're crazy," Kendall said angrily. "Stark raving mad. You won't get a better offer. And you won't get me to increase mine, if that's what you're thinking. Take it or leave it."

"I'll leave it," Bob said. "Even if I have to sell, Mr. Kendall, I'd prefer not to sell to somebody who wants to develop the land. I happen to believe that Compton's better off without a big supermarket here and I don't want to get involved in anybody's get-rich-quick schemes."

While Bob was speaking, Philip Kendall's face had slowly turned purple. Neil wanted to burst out laughing, but in another way it was quite alarming to watch. He had the awful feeling that Kendall might explode. And when he spoke, the words came out in a splutter, like a fast-deflating balloon. "It's all perfectly legal, you know. It's for the good of the town. You've no right to —"

"No, Mr. Kendall," Bob said. "This is *my* property and I have every right. Good afternoon."

Kendall turned to Carole. "Can't you talk some sense into him?" he said furiously.

"I think I already did," Carole replied. "I don't want to sell, either. I'm sorry, Mr. Kendall, but I think you'd better leave."

"I'll give you another ten thousand and that's my last offer!"

Carole just shook her head. Neil thought she was starting to look annoyed. From somewhere near his feet he heard a low growling. Sam was too well trained to leave Neil's side but even he was showing a dislike for Philip Kendall.

"You'd better keep that dog away from me!" Kendall said, glaring at Neil. He started to back away and then turned and walked rapidly to the gate. Sam never moved, but he barked loudly to speed Kendall on his way.

Neil heard the BMW start up and the crunching of its wheels on the gravel. "That was great!" he gasped and started laughing.

"We won't see him again," Carole said. "I hope."

"Dad," Neil asked, recovering his composure, "does this mean you won't sell at all?"

Bob let out a long sigh. "I don't know," he said. "It all depends —"

He broke off what he was going to say as Sarah

came running out of the house, calling, "Daddy! Daddy! There's a phone call for you!"

"Another member of your fan club," Carole said dryly.

Bob grinned at her and went into the house with Sarah. Neil set off in search of Emily to tell her the good news and waved good-bye to Kate, who was going home. He found Emily in the rescue center changing the water in Blackie's dish.

"I wish I'd been there," Emily said when she heard the news about Kendall's hasty departure. "Did you ask him what he was doing last Thursday night?"

"You mean, was he setting fire to the barn? Don't be an idiot! He'd have gone ballistic."

"Well, I want to know," Emily said determinedly.

Neil wanted to know, too, but he still couldn't think of any way of finding out. If Kendall had been responsible for the fire, he was never going to admit it. And Neil could hardly walk up to Old Mill Farm and start asking questions.

All of that was swept out of his head when he and Emily walked into the kitchen a couple of minutes later. Bob and Carole were standing in stony silence. Bob's face was white, and he looked the most unhappy that Neil had ever seen him. Neil knew something serious was wrong.

"That was Mike Turner on the phone," he said in a somber voice. He sounded shaken. "We've got to go over right away. It's . . . Red's dying."

CHAPTER NINE

Mike Turner met Bob, Neil, and Emily on the steps of his animal hospital in Compton. He looked anxious and unhappy. "I'm sorry," he said as they approached the double doors and he waved them inside. "I can't tell you how sorry I am. It's an infection. His temperature has been rising since this morning, and he didn't like it when I touched his stomach. The pain will be getting worse. I gave him a blood test just to be sure. . . ."

"And what did it show?" Neil asked nervously.

"It's peritonitis."

"Isn't there any cure for it?" Emily asked in dismay.

Mike shook his head. "It's a risk when there are internal injuries. I'm afraid that once it takes hold there's nothing I can do. I gave him a shot of the strongest antibiotic we've got. But he's not responding. He collapsed just before I called you."

Mike showed the Parkers into the intensive care unit.

When Neil had last seen Red he had shown signs of looking more alert, as if he was starting to come back to life again. Now he lay still on the mat in his cage. He was back on the IV drip and the only movement was the uneven rise and fall of his chest in time with the sound of his labored breathing. Bob went over and gently rubbed his muzzle.

"Red," he said.

Neil clenched his hands. He could feel his fingernails driving into his palms. He wanted to say, "Come on, Red, you're a fighter, you can do it," but there was no way the words would come out past the lump in his throat. Next to him, Emily stood silently.

"There's nothing more I can do for Red," Mike said. He went out and closed the door softly behind him. It was a sign that Mike knew Red didn't have much longer.

Bob went on caressing the setter's head, not saying another word, looking down at him with a face devoid of expression. He was steeling himself for the inevitable.

Afterward, Neil was never sure how long they stood there, listening to Red's hoarse breathing. There was a pause between each breath, as if there would never be another, and it was a relief every time there was.

Then, without warning, a shiver rippled through the dog's body. Red's paws twitched. He tried to raise his head and drew two or three harsh, irregular breaths. Bob reached down and tried to support him, but Red went limp in his arms.

"No!" Emily cried. "Oh, no!" There were tears on her face.

Bob let out a long sigh and closed his eyes. His hand stroked Red's shining flank and then he laid him down and moved away.

Neil wiped his eyes. He hadn't realized until then that he was crying, too. The night of the fire flooded back into his mind. He remembered being in the barn, groping around in fire and darkness as he tried to find the way out, coughing in the smoke-filled air. He remembered the relief as he heard Red's bark, and felt the tug on his jacket leading him to safety. Neil reached out and stroked Red's gleaming coat for the last time. The beautiful setter's body was still warm.

"I wouldn't be here if it wasn't for Red," he whispered. Neil felt his father wrap an arm around his shoulder.

"He was a good dog," Bob said and they stood quietly together. After a few painful moments, Bob went to the door and called for his friend.

*   *   *

The vet came back and gave Red a cursory examination. "I'm really sorry, Bob," he said. After a minute, he added, "Do you want to bury him here?" Mike Turner had a pet cemetery, under the trees in the small garden attached to the hospital.

Bob shook his head. "No, thanks, Mike. Red was my dog. Did I tell you Jim Birchall had left him to me? I want to take him home."

Neil got a blanket from the car. Bob wrapped Red in it and carried him outside. Emily clutched at Neil's hand as they followed behind, and for once Neil didn't mind. Bob laid Red in the back of the car, shook hands with Mike, and got into the driver's seat. Neil and Emily climbed in, and Bob drove off.

Neil's stomach was churning. He couldn't think straight. He couldn't believe they were never going to see Red again — his bright eyes, his friendly, eager face. He'd been ready to welcome Red into the family at King Street Kennels. He couldn't believe that it wasn't going to happen.

But he had to think about his father, too. Until now Neil had expected that it was all going to turn out fine. Bob had refused Mr. Kendall's offer. Even if the insurance company didn't pay to rebuild the barn, there were other ways of starting up again. His dad had started to fight back, to become the person Neil had always known and loved. His smile had returned. But would he want to go on fighting now that Red had died?

The Range Rover pulled up outside King Street Kennels before Neil had even noticed they were on their way home. Feeling as if he were lifting an enormous weight, Neil roused himself and got out of the car. At the same moment, the door of the house flew open and Carole came running out.

"Bob, is he . . ."

Bob went to meet her and Carole, seeing the answer in his face, put her arms around him. "I'm sorry, love."

Neil opened the back of the car where Red lay wrapped in the blanket.

"We'll bury him in the field," Bob told him. "In the open. It's where he liked to be."

"I'll help," Neil said. "I'll get a couple of spades." He walked off toward the garden shed where the tools were kept.

Sarah was sitting at the kitchen table. Emily guessed that her mom must have told her where they were all going because her eyes were red and her face was puffy from crying. In front of her was a picture of Red that she had been painting while they were away.

When Neil appeared at the kitchen door with two spades, Sarah started to cry again. Carole sat beside her and comforted her as best she could.

Bob Parker took a long sip from the cup of tea that Carole had made him and looked at Neil standing in the doorway, his expression so sad. "I wonder what Jim Birchall would think if he knew his dog was dead. He trusted me to look after him."

"You did your best. And Red died a hero," Carole said, with an arm around Sarah. "He brought Neil out of the barn."

"Dad," said Neil. "You know Mr. Birchall left you some money to look after Red. Could that go toward rebuilding the barn?"

Bob shook his head. "No, it wouldn't feel right. Anyway, I'm not sure if I'd be allowed to."

"Then use it for the rescue center," said Emily.

"No." Bob thought for a minute. "No, I don't think we should take the money at all after what's happened. I'll go to see Jim's lawyer, and if he agrees I'll give the money to the SPCA."

There was a short silence. Everybody, Neil could see, thought that was the right thing to do.

"But you are going to rebuild the barn, Dad?" he asked. "We are staying here, aren't we?"

Bob opened his mouth to reply but the sound of the doorbell denied them all his answer.

"What next?" Carole said, raising her eyes to the ceiling.

"I'll go," said Emily.

When she opened the front door, her heart sank. Standing on the step was Mr. Pye from the insurance company.

CHAPTER TEN

"**D**ad!" Emily called out.

Bob Parker came out of the kitchen and along the hall. He stopped in his tracks when he saw who the visitor was. "Mr. Pye. You'd better come in."

Mr. Pye wiped his polished shoes on the mat. There was nothing in his sour expression to show why he had come. Bob showed him into the kitchen, and Emily followed them.

"Oh . . ." Carole said as they arrived. She got up from the table. "Bob, wouldn't it be better to talk in the office?"

Bob looked confused. Neil knew that his father's mind was still focused on Red, not on what the insurance man had to say.

"Please don't trouble yourself," said Mr. Pye. "I

can't stay long." He shook hands with Carole. "Mrs. Parker? How are you?"

"Please sit down," said Carole, motioning toward a chair.

"Thank you." Mr. Pye hitched up his pant legs and sat down. Everybody, even Sam, was looking at him as if he were going to bite. Neil felt himself relax a little. If Mr. Pye was going to accuse his father of burning down the barn on purpose, he would hardly be sitting at their kitchen table while he delivered the bomb.

"I thought you would like to know," Mr. Pye began, "that the insurance investigators have completed their report on your barn and their findings concur with those of the local authorities. A copy of our own findings will be in the mail to you tomorrow, but I thought you would like to know as soon as possible." He paused for a few moments. Neil thought he might be enjoying the suspense, and the man actually managed a frosty little smile. "You have nothing more to worry about, Mr. Parker."

The tension in Bob's body seemed to melt and his shoulders relaxed.

"The fire started because of a fault in the electrical wiring that supplies artificial light to said building. You could say it was like a bomb ticking away inside the wall. Nobody could have known about it, and nobody is to blame."

"That's wonderful!" said Carole.

Neil felt a wave of relief wash over him.

Even Bob was smiling.

"So it wasn't Mr. Kendall," Emily said to Neil in a low voice.

Neil thought she sounded disappointed. She really had it in for Philip Kendall! But the man wasn't a criminal, after all — just a businessman out for a profit and unscrupulously taking advantage of their misfortune. It still didn't make Neil like him any better, though. "So what happens now?" he asked.

"The insurance payment should come through within the next few days," Mr. Pye said. "It should completely cover the cost of replacing the building and compensate you for any other damage to the property as a direct result of this tragedy. You can begin clearing the site as soon as you like. And I'll send a copy of the report to the council."

"Thank you, Mr. Pye," said Bob. "You've taken a load off our minds. It's really nice of you to come around and tell us like this."

Mr. Pye stood up. "Think nothing of it," he said. "Please, if there's anything more you want to know, don't hesitate to get in touch."

He shook hands again with Carole, and Bob showed him out.

"Awesome!" said Emily, her eyes shining.

"That was kind of Mr. Pye," Carole said. "Neil, I thought you told me he was horrible."

Neil looked away and shrugged. "Did I?"

"We shouldn't have any problems with the council now," Carole added with satisfaction.

"And we won't have to give up the kennel!" Neil felt as if he wanted to jump up and start singing. "Mom, we are staying, aren't we?"

"We are," Bob said firmly as he reappeared at the kitchen door. "I can tell Eddie Thomas to go ahead with the barn — and pay him the proper price."

Neil and Emily cheered loudly. Sarah wiped her damp eyes and cried out, "Yippee!"

"This means Mr. Kendall won't spoil Compton with a huge supermarket!" Emily added.

The doorbell rang again and Neil just managed to hear it above the commotion. He darted out of the kitchen to answer it and came back a moment later with Eddie Thomas.

"What's the occasion?" said Eddie, smiling and ushering into the room a small woman wearing a brightly colored scarf. "Can anyone join in?"

"Hello there, Eddie," Bob said. "I've just had some good news. The insurance company is going to pay for our new barn. You can come by as soon as you like to get started!"

"That's great!" Eddie said, grinning. "But that's not what I've come about." He put a hand on the woman's arm. "This is my wife, Maureen. Maureen, welcome to King Street Kennels!"

Maureen and Bob shook hands.

"It's about the little dog," Maureen said. "When

Eddie told me about her, I thought we just had to come over and see her. She hasn't gone yet, has she?"

Bob smiled. "No, she hasn't. To be honest, I had a sneaking suspicion that Eddie would decide to take her."

"It's me who does the deciding around our house," Maureen said, looking at her husband with a twinkle in her eye.

Eddie sighed. "What a tyrant she is!" he said.

There was never any doubt that Blackie had found a new home. As soon as they opened the door of the puppy's pen in the rescue center, the little black dog hurled herself at Maureen and was scooped up into her arms. Maureen laughed as Blackie licked her face enthusiastically.

"Do you charge for adoptions?" Eddie asked.

"No," said Carole, "but we accept donations to help cover our running costs. There's no pressure about that, though."

"That shouldn't be a problem. Business is good at the moment," Eddie told her. "I just got a new job!"

Before Eddie and Maureen left, Bob gave them some nutritional information for Blackie.

"You'll have to tell us what to do," Eddie said. "We've never had a dog before."

"We always keep track of how our rescue dogs are doing," Bob said, "so I guess we'll be seeing a lot of each other, what with you working on the barn as

well. When she's old enough, you might like to bring her to my obedience classes."

Neil and Emily looked at each other. This was the first time their father had mentioned starting up the classes again.

"Twice a week, Wednesday evening and Sunday morning," Bob explained. "I used to hold them in the barn, but while the weather stays nice I'm going to use the field."

"Great!" Eddie said. "Count us in when the time comes."

Neil watched Eddie and Maureen as they climbed back into Eddie's dirty white van. Blackie was squirming ecstatically in Maureen's arms, and all three of them looked delighted to have found each other. Neil began to believe that everything was going to be all right. As they walked back into the kitchen after all their excitement, Neil noticed the two spades propped up against the wall. If it hadn't been for Red's death, everything would have been perfect.

The Parkers buried Red under a hawthorn tree in one of the hedges bordering the exercise field. The sun was going down as Bob and Carole dug the grave. Meanwhile Neil and Emily made a marker with Red's name on it. Sarah pinned her picture of Red, carefully covered in thick, clear plastic, to the tree above the grave.

Neil watched as Bob replaced the grass on top of the soil, and Emily arranged some flowers.

"Good-bye, Red," Neil murmured. "You saved my life. I'll never forget you." He realized that it was almost a week since he had seen Red racing across the grass while Bob threw sticks for him to fetch. He remembered Red running toward them, with the sun reflecting off his shiny coat. Perhaps, in a way, he would always be there.

He reached down to where Sam sat quietly beside him and rumpled the Border collie's ears. The touch of the warm coat was comforting. As if he knew that Neil needed him, Sam turned his head and nuzzled Neil's hand.

For a few minutes everyone stood in silence, looking down at the little grass-covered mound where Red was buried.

"None of us will forget him," Bob said as they turned away and started to walk back to the house.

Halfway there, a thought came to Neil. He stopped.

"Dad," he said. "When the barn's built again, why don't we call it Red's Barn? Then everybody will remember him, not just us."

Bob stopped and faced him.

"That's a good idea, Neil. A very good idea." As he walked on, Neil heard him repeating softly, "Red's Barn."

They filed through the field gate into the garden.

"Dinner in half an hour," Carole said, taking Sarah's hand and leading her back to the house. "Your dad's cooking!"

Neil and Emily were about to follow when Bob said, "Neil, what have you been doing about Brownie?"

Neil could hardly believe what his father had just said, but he managed to stop himself from gaping. "Kate and I worked with him," he said, "but he doesn't want to come to either of us. He's too scared. And when he's scared, he wants to bite."

Bob shook his head. "That'll never do," he said. "We'll never find him a new owner in that state."

"I know. I'm sorry, Dad. We did our best."

Bob smiled at him. "I'm sure you did. Come on, show me."

He strode off toward the rescue center. Emily made a thumbs-up sign to Neil as they followed. It had been a tough week, but it was all over now. The Puppy Patrol was back in business!